Beaver is lost.

BEAVER IS LOST

ELISHA COOPER

schwartz & wade books · new york

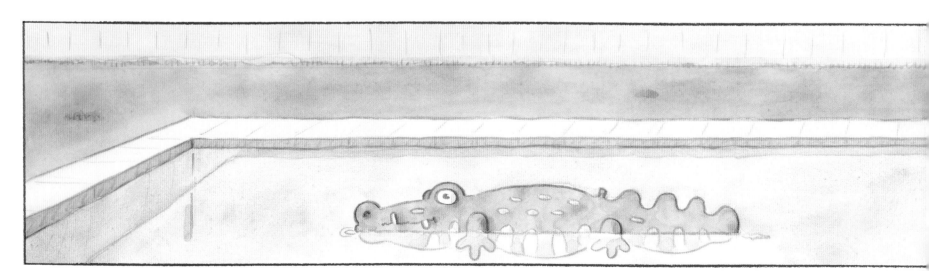

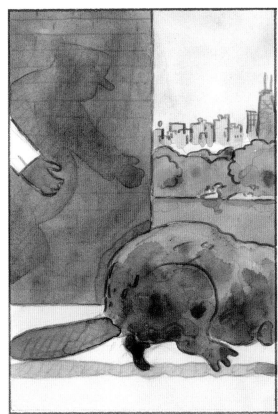

Home.

All rights reserved. Published in the United States by Schwartz & Wade Books,
an imprint of Random House Children's Books, a division of Random House, Inc., New York.

Schwartz & Wade Books and the colophon are trademarks of Random House, Inc.

Visit us on the Web! www.randomhouse.com/kids

Educators and librarians, for a variety of teaching tools,
visit us at www.randomhouse.com/teachers

*Library of Congress Cataloging-in-Publication Data*

Cooper, Elisha.
Beaver is lost / Elisha Cooper. — 1st ed.
p. cm.
Summary: A lost beaver looks for the way home.
ISBN 978-0-375-85765-2 (trade) — ISBN 978-0-375-95765-9 (glb)
1. Beavers—Juvenile fiction. [1. Beavers—Fiction.] I. Title.
PZ10.3.C779 Be 2010
[E]—dc22
2009024915

The text of this book is set in Weiss.
The illustrations are rendered in watercolor and pencil.
Book design by Rachael Cole
MANUFACTURED IN CHINA

10 9 8 7 6 5 4 3 2 1

First Edition

For Zoë and Mia